FÜN學美國小學科

Preschool 閱讀課本 二版

AMERiCAN SCHOOL TEXTBOOK

Reading Key

Preschool

動詞篇

1

MP3

寂天雲 APP

作者 ◎ Michael A. Putlack &
e-Creative Contents

譯者 ◎ 歐寶妮

如何下載 MP3 音檔

❶ 寂天雲 APP 聆聽：掃描書上 QR Code 下載
「寂天雲－英日語學習隨身聽」APP。加入會員
後，用 APP 內建掃描器再次掃描書上 QR
Code，即可使用 APP 聆聽音檔。

❷ 官網下載音檔：請上「寂天閱讀網」
（www.icosmos.com.tw），註冊會員／登入後，
搜尋本書，進入本書頁面，點選「MP3 下載」
下載音檔，存於電腦等其他播放器聆聽使用。

Authors

Michael A. Putlack
Michael A. Putlack graduated from Tufts University in Medford, Massachusetts, USA, where he got his B.A. in History and English and his M.A. in History. He has written a number of books for children, teenagers, and adults.

e-Creative Contents
A creative group that develops English contents and products for ESL and EFL students.

The Best Preparation for Building Basic Vocabulary and Grammar

The Reading Key — Preschool series is designed to help children understand basic words and grammar to learn English. This series also helps children develop their reading skills in a fun and easy way.

Features

- Learning high-frequency words that appear in all kinds of reading material
- Building basic grammar and reading comprehension skills to learn English
- Various activities including reading and writing practice
- A wide variety of topics that cover American school subjects
- Full-color photographs and illustrations

The Reading Key series has five levels.

- Reading Key **Preschool 1–6**
  a six-book series designed for preschoolers and kindergarteners

- Reading Key **Basic 1–4**
  a four-book series designed for kindergarteners and beginners

- Reading Key **Volume 1–3**
  a three-book series designed for beginner to intermediate learners

- Reading Key **Volume 4–6**
  a three-book series designed for intermediate to high-intermediate learners

- Reading Key **Volume 7–9**
  a three-book series designed for high-intermediate learners

Table of Contents | Preschool 1 Verbs

Components Workbook for Daily Review • Answers and Translations

Syllabus | Preschool 1 Verbs

Subject	Unit	Grammar	Vocabulary
Be Verbs & Have, Has	**Unit 1** I Am, I Have	**Present simple:** am, have	• I, am, have • Animals' names and features
	Unit 2 He Is, He Has	**Present simple:** is, has	• he, she, it, boy, girl, is, has • Animals' names and features
	Unit 3 I Am Running	**Present continuous:** be + V-ing	• walking, running, flying, swimming • singing, dancing • cooking, eating • I see
	Unit 4 You Are Sleeping	**Present continuous:** be + V-ing	• I, you, we, they, are • drinking, eating • sleeping, jumping
Common Verbs	**Unit 5** I Run	**Present simple:** I/You/They/We run	• run, walk, swim, jump • well, fast, slowly • I like to
	Unit 6 She Runs	**Present simple:** He/She/It runs	• runs, sings, dances, swims, eats • She likes to
	Unit 7 Go, Went	**Past simple:** Regular and irregular verbs	• today, yesterday • eat/ate, go/went, do/did, come/came, see/saw, play/played
	Unit 8 Will, Be Going to	**Future tense:** will, be going to	• today, tomorrow • play soccer, play baseball, play a game, play with friends, ride a bike, watch TV, have a party

I Am, I Have

🎧 01 **Key Words** Read the words.

mane

trunk

lion

elephant

neck

mouth

giraffe

hippo

I am Jane.
Who are you?

I am a lion.

I am a giraffe.

I am a hippo.

I am an elephant.

I Have

(Circle) the word **have**.

I have two hands.

I have two eyes.

I have two ears.

I have two legs.

I have four legs!

Am or Have?

Circle the correct word for each sentence.

I am a lion.
I (**am**, **have**) a mane.

I am a giraffe.
I (**am**, **have**) a long neck.

I am an elephant.
I (**am**, **have**) a trunk.

I am a hippo.
I (**am**, **have**) a big mouth.

Who Am I?

Draw lines to match the sentences with each animal.

I have four legs.
I have a long neck.

elephant

I have four legs.
I have a trunk.

lion

I have four legs.
I have a mane.

giraffe

I have four legs.
I have a big mouth.

hippo

I Can Read

Read the story. (Circle) the correct word for each sentence.

Animals in Africa

I am an elephant.
I have a (**trunk**, **mane**).

I am a lion.
I have a (**mane**, **trunk**).

I am a hippo.
I have a big (**mouth, mane**).

I am a giraffe.
I have a long (**neck, trunk**).

He Is, He Has

 Key Words Read the words.

boy = he

girl = she

bird

rabbit

it

dog

cat

He Is, She Is, It Is

Circle the word **is**.

The boy is Tom.

He **is** John.

The girl **is** Jane.

She **is** Julie.

It **is** a bird.

16

He Has, She Has, It Has

Circle the word **has**.

The girl has a cat.
She **has** a cat.

The boy **has** a dog.
He **has** a dog.

The girl **has** a rabbit.
She **has** a rabbit.

The boy **has** a bird.
He **has** a bird.

The bird **has** two wings.
It **has** two wings.

Have or Has?

Circle the correct word for each sentence.

Jane

Tom

Who has the cat?
Jane (**have**, **has**) the cat.

Who has the dog?
Tom (**have**, **has**) the dog.

Who has the rabbit?
Julie (**have**, **has**) the rabbit.

Who has the bird?
John (**have**, **has**) the bird.

Julie

John

(11) # What Is It?

Draw a line to match the sentence with each animal.

Unit 2 — He Is, He Has

▼ It has big eyes.

▼ It has a big mouth.

▼ It has two wings.

▼ It has long ears.

It is a hippo.

It is a cat.

It is a rabbit.

It is a bird.

19

I Can Read

Read the story. Circle the correct word for each sentence.

Animal Friends

(She, He) is Jane.
She has a cat.
It has big eyes.

(She, He) is Jake.
He has a dog.
It has big ears.

She is Anna.
She (**has**, **have**) a bird.
It has two wings.

He is Tom.
He has a rabbit.
It (**has**, **have**) long ears.

21

I Am Running

Key Words Read the words.

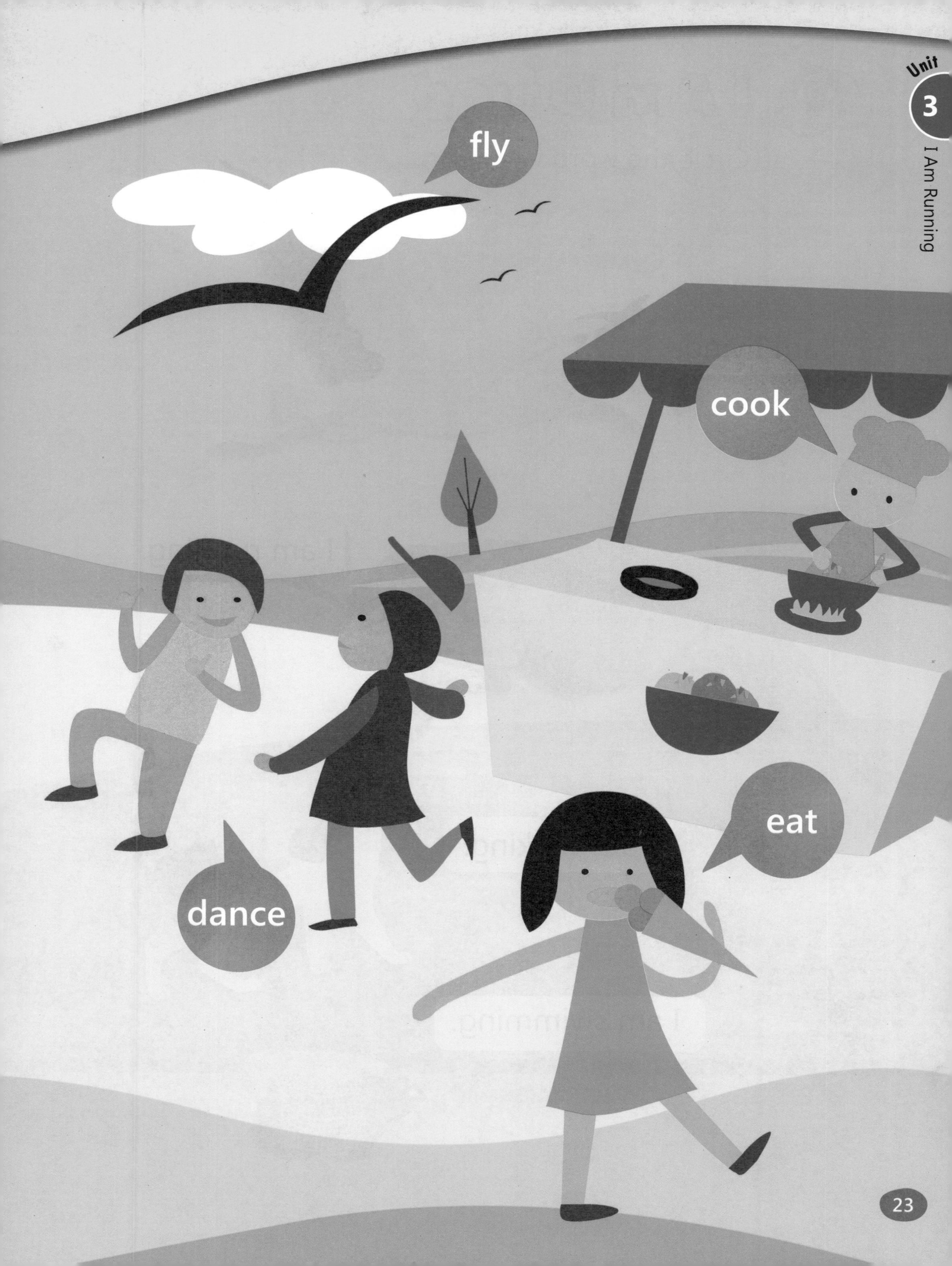
fly
cook
dance
eat

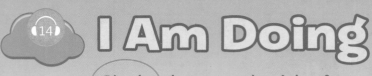

I Am Doing

Circle the word with **-ing**.

I am (flying).

I am running.

I am walking.

I am swimming.

What Are You Doing?

Circle the correct word for each sentence.

I am a bird.
I am (**swimming**, **flying**).

I am a cat.
I am (**walking**, **running**).

I am a dog.
I am (**walking**, **running**).

I am a fish.
I am (**swimming**, **flying**).

Fill in the blanks with the words from the box.

walking   running   swimming   flying

I see a lion.
The lion is walking .

I see a zebra.
The zebra is _____.

I see a hippo.
The hippo is _____.

I see a bird.
The bird is _____.

Singing or Sing?

Circle the correct word for each sentence.

I see a girl.
The girl is (singing, sing).

I see a boy.
The boy is (dancing, dance).

I see Mom.
Mom is (cook, cooking).

I see Tom.
He is (eat, eating).

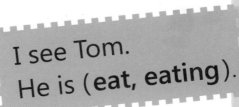

I Can Read

Read the story. (Circle) the correct word for each sentence.

What is Ann **doing**?
She is (**singing**, **swimming**).

What is Tom **doing**?
He is (**dancing**, **running**).

What is Mom **doing?**
She is (**flying, cooking**).

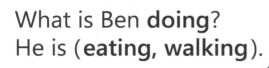

What is Ben **doing**?
He is (**eating, walking**).

You Are Sleeping

Key Words Read the words.

I

you

we

he

she

they

eat

drink

sleep

jump

You Are, They Are

Circle the words **in blue**.

I am **Ann.**

You are **Tom.**

We are friends.

He is **a boy.**

She is **a girl.**

They are **children.**

You Are Doing

21

Circle the words with **-ing**.

I am eating.

You are drinking.

We are jumping.

They are sleeping.

I am Ann.
I am (**eating**, **drinking**) pizza.

You are Tom.
You are (**eating**, **drinking**) milk.

We are good friends.
We are (**jumping**, **sleeping**) together.

They are children.
They are (**jumping**, **sleeping**).

What Are They Doing?

Circle the correct word for each sentence.

I see lions.
They are (**sleeping**, **jumping**).

I see kangaroos.
They are (**sleeping**, **jumping**).

I see giraffes.
They are (**eating**, **drinking**) grass.

I see elephants.
They are (**eating**, **drinking**) water.

I Can Read

Read the story. (Circle) the correct word for each sentence.

What are you **doing**?
I am (**eat,** **eating**) ice cream.

What are you **doing**?
I am (**drink, drinking**) milk.

What are they **doing**?
They are (**sleep, sleeping**).

What are they **doing**?
They are (**jump, jumping**) rope.

A Choose and write.

legs   eyes   ears   neck   mane   trunk

1. eyes

2.

3.

4.

5.

6.

B Circle the correct word.

1.

I (**am**, **are**) Jane.

2.

You (**am**, **are**) Tom.

3.

She (**is**, **are**) a girl.

4.

He (**is**, **are**) a boy.

5.

It (**is**, **are**) a cat.

6.

They (**is**, **are**) children.

C Circle the correct word.

1.

I am Julie.
I (**have**, **has**) two hands.

2.

You are a bird.
You (**have**, **has**) two wings.

3.

She is Ann.
She (**have**, **has**) a dog.

4.

It is an elephant.
It (**have**, **has**) a trunk.

D Read and match.

1. I see lions.
   They are sleeping.

2. I see giraffes.
   They are eating grass.

3. I see a girl.
   She is eating a sandwich.

4. I see a boy.
   He is drinking water.

5

I Run

 Key Words

Read the words and sentences.

rabbit

turtle

frog

dolphin

I run.

You walk.

We jump.

They swim.

Who Are You?

Circle the words **in blue**.

You are **a turtle.**

I am a rabbit.

They are **dolphins.**

We are **frogs.**

42

Run, Jump, Swim

Circle the words **in blue**.

I am a rabbit.
I run fast.

You are a turtle.
You walk slowly.

We are frogs.
We jump well.

They are dolphins.
They swim well.

Sing, Dance

Circle the correct word for each sentence.

I am a singer.
I (**sing, dance**) well.

You are a dancer.
You (**sing, dance**) well.

We are singers.
We (**sing, dance**) well.

They are dancers.
They (**sing, dance**) well.

 **I Like to**

Draw a line to match each picture and the sentence.

I like to sing.

● - - - - - - - - - - ● I am a singer.

I like to dance.

● ● I am a dancer.

I like to swim.

● ● I am a frog.

I like to jump.

● ● I am a dolphin.

I Can Read

Read the story. Circle the correct word for each sentence.

Who Am I?

I like to dance.
I dance well.
I am a (**dancer**, **singer**).

I like to sing.
I sing well.
I am a (**singer, dancer**).

I like to run.
I (**run, swim**) fast.
I am a horse.

I like to swim.
I (**swim, run**) well.
I am a fish.

UNIT 6

She Runs

 Key Words

Read the words and sentences.

she

he

it

48

She runs.

It runs.

He sings.

It sings.

I See

Circle the words **in blue**.

I see a girl.
She sings well.

I see a boy.
He **dances** well.

I see a dolphin.
It **swims** fast.

I see a horse.
It **runs** fast.

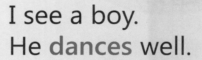

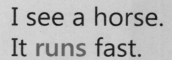

Sings, Dances

Circle the correct word for each sentence.

The girl sings.
She (**sing**, **sings**) well.

The boy dances.
He (**dance**, **dances**) well.

The horse runs.
It (**run**, **runs**) fast.

The dolphin swims.
It (**swim**, **swims**) fast.

She Likes to

Draw a line to match the sentence with each picture.

She likes to walk. •   •

He likes to run. •   •

She likes to swim. •   •

He likes to sleep. •   •

It likes to jump. •   •

Who Are They?

Circle the correct word for each sentence.

She is Jane.
She (**like**, **likes**) to walk.

He is Tom.
He (**like**, **likes**) to run.

The girl is Ann.
She (**like**, **likes**) to swim.

It is a cat.
It (**like**, **likes**) to sleep.

It is a frog.
It (**like**, **likes**) to jump.

I Can Read

Read the story. (Circle) the correct word for each sentence.

Meet My Friend

I have a dog.
His name is Sam.

He likes to run.
He (**run**, **runs**) fast.

He likes to jump.
He (**jump, jumps**) well.

He likes to dance.
He (**dance, dances**) well.

He likes to eat.
He (**eat, eats**) well.
He is fun.

UNIT 7 Go, Went

Key Words Read the words.

school

park

movie

party

come home

do homework

play baseball

Eat, Ate

Circle the word **eat**. Underline the word **ate**.

Today	Yesterday
 I eat an apple.	 I ate an apple.
 I eat a banana.	 I ate a banana.
 I eat a sandwich.	 I ate a sandwich.
 I eat a cookie.	 I ate a cookie.

Eat or Ate?

Circle the correct word for each sentence.

Today, I eat an apple.
Yesterday, I (**eat, ate**) an apple, too.

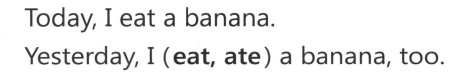

Today, I eat a banana.
Yesterday, I (**eat, ate**) a banana, too.

Today, I eat a sandwich.
Yesterday, I (**eat, ate**) a sandwich, too.

Today, I eat a cookie.
Yesterday, I (**eat, ate**) a cookie, too.

Go, Went

Circle the word **go**. Underline the word **went**.

Today	Yesterday

I (go) to school.  I went to school.

I go to the park.  I went to the park.

I go to a movie.  I went to a movie.

I go to a party.  I went to a party.

60

Go or Went?

Circle the correct word for each sentence.

Today, I go to school.
Yesterday, I (**go,** **went**) to school, too.

Today, I go to the park.
Yesterday, I (**go, went**) to the park, too.

Today, I go to a movie.
Yesterday, I (**go, went**) to a movie, too.

Today, I go to a party.
Yesterday, I (**go, went**) to a party, too.

Do, Did

Circle the words **in blue**. Underline the words **in red**.

Today		Yesterday

I do my homework.   I did my homework.

I come home early.   I came home early.

I see a bird.   I saw a bird.

I play baseball.   I played baseball.

Do or Did?

Circle the correct word for each sentence.

Today, I do my homework.
Yesterday, I (**do,** **did**) my homework, too.

Today, I come home early.
Yesterday, I (**come, came**) home early, too.

Today, I see a bird.
Yesterday, I (**see, saw**) a bird, too.

Today, I play baseball.
Yesterday, I (**play, played**) baseball, too.

I Can Read

Read the story. Circle the words **in blue**.

Yesterday, I was busy.

I went to school.

I went to the park.

UNIT

8

Will, Be Going to

 Key Words Read the words.

play soccer

play baseball

play a game

play with friends

ride a bike

watch TV

have a party

 **I Will** (Circle) the word **will**.

Today

Tomorrow

I play soccer.

I (will) play soccer.

I play baseball.

I will play baseball.

I ride a bike.

I will ride a bike.

I watch TV.

I will watch TV.

What Will You Do?

(Circle) the word **will**.

Today, I play soccer.
Tomorrow, I (will) play soccer, too.

Today, you play baseball.
Tomorrow, you will play baseball, too.

Today, we ride a bike.
Tomorrow, we will ride a bike, too.

Today, they watch TV.
Tomorrow, they will watch TV, too.

I Am Going to

Circle the words **am going to** and **are going to**.

Today		Tomorrow
I go to school.		I (am going to) go to school.
I go to the park.		I am going to go to the park.
You play a game.		You are going to play a game.
You play with your friends.		You are going to play with your friends.

What Are You Going to Do?

Circle the correct word for each sentence.

Today, I go to school.
Tomorrow, I (**am**, **are**) going to
go to school, too.

Today, I ride a bike.
Tomorrow, I am (**go**, **going**) to
ride a bike, too.

Today, you play a game.
Tomorrow, you are (**go**, **going**) to
play a game, too.

Today, you play with your friends.
Tomorrow, you are going to
(**play**, **played**) with your friends, too.

I Can Read

Read the story. Circle the words **will** and **are going to**.

My Birthday Party

Tomorrow is my birthday.
I will have a party.

My friends will come to my party.
Jane will come to my party.
Tina will come to my party.
Ben will come to my party, too.

We are going to eat cake.

We are going to eat pizza.

We are going to eat ice cream.

We are going to play a game, too.

The party will be fun.

Review Test 2

A Choose and write.

jump   run   swim   walk   dance   sing

1. run

 2.

3.

 4.

5.

 6.

B Circle the correct word.

1.

I ((run), runs) fast.

2.

You (**walk**, **walks**) slowly.

3.

We (**sing**, **sings**) well.

4.

They (**dance**, **dances**) well.

5.

He (**jump**, **jumps**) well.

6.

It (**swim**, **swims**) fast.

74

C Circle the correct word.

1.

   I (**like, likes**) to dance.
   I am a dancer.

2.

   You (**like, likes**) to sing.
   You are a singer.

3.

   He (**like, likes**) to run.
   He runs fast.

4.

   It (**like, likes**) to swim.
   It swims well.

D Choose and match.

1. Today, I come home early.
   Yesterday, I (**come, came**)
   home early, too.

2. Today, I see a bird.
   Yesterday, I (**see, saw**)
   a bird, too.

3. Today, I play soccer.
   Tomorrow, I will
   (**play, played**) soccer, too.

4. Today, I eat cake.
   Tomorrow, I am going to
   (**eat, ate**) cake, too.

Word List

Unit 1

I Am, I Have
我是，我有

1 **lion** 獅子

2 **mane** 鬃毛

3 **elephant** 大象

4 **trunk** 象鼻

5 **giraffe** 長頸鹿

6 **neck** 脖子

7 **long neck** 長脖子

8 **hippo** 河馬

9 **mouth** 嘴巴

10 **big mouth** 大嘴巴

11 **I am** 我是

12 **I have** 我有

13 **who** 誰

14 **Who are you?** 你是誰？

15 **hand** 手 *two hands 兩隻手

16 **leg** 腳 *two legs 兩隻腳

17 **eye** 眼睛 *two eyes 兩隻眼睛

18 **ear** 耳朵 *two ears 兩隻耳朵

19 **Who am I?** 我是誰？

20 **animal** 動物 *複數：animals 動物們

21 **in Africa** 在非洲

Unit 2

He Is, He Has
他是，他有

1 **boy** 男孩

2 **he** 他

3 **girl** 女孩

4 **she** 她

5 **cat** 貓

6 **dog** 狗

7 **rabbit** 兔子

8 **bird** 鳥

9 **it** 牠；它

10 **He is** 他是

11 **She is** 她是

12 **It is** 它是

13 **He has** 他有

14 **She has** 她有

15 **It has** 牠有；它有

16 **wing** 翅膀

　　*two wings 兩隻翅膀

Unit 3

I Am Running
我正在跑步

1 **walk** 走路

2 **run** 跑步

3 **fly** 飛

4 **swim** 游泳

5 **sing** 唱歌

6 **dance** 跳舞

7 **cook** 烹飪

8 **eat** 吃

9 **doing** 正在做……

10 **I am doing** 我正在做……

11 **walking** 正在走路

12 **running** 正在跑步

13 **flying** 正在飛

14 **swimming** 正在游泳

15 **what** 什麼（疑問代名詞）

16 **What are you doing?**
你正在做什麼？

17 **fish** 魚

18 **see** 看見

19 **zebra** 斑馬

20 **Mom** 媽媽

21 **What is Ann doing?**
安正在做什麼？

Unit 4

You Are Sleeping
你正在睡覺

1 **I** 我

2 **you** 你

3 **we** 我們

4 **he** 他

5 **she** 她

6 **they** 他（她）們；牠們

7 **eat** 吃

8 **drink** 喝

9 **sleep** 睡

10 **jump** 跳

11 **You are** 你是

12 **They are** 他（她）們是；牠們是

13 **We are** 我們是

14 **friend** 朋友 *複數：friends 朋友們

15 **children** 孩子們

16 **eating** 正在吃

17 **drinking** 正在喝

18 **jumping** 正在跳

19 **sleeping** 正在睡

20 **drink milk** 喝牛奶

21	together	一起
22	eat grass	吃草
23	drink water	喝水
24	jump rope	跳繩

Unit 5

I Run 我跑

1	rabbit	兔子
2	turtle	烏龜
3	frog	青蛙
4	dolphin	海豚
5	run	跑
6	walk	走
7	jump	跳
8	swim	游泳
9	Who are you?	你是誰？
10	fast	快；迅速
11	slowly	緩慢地
12	well	很好地
13	sing	唱歌
14	dance	跳舞
15	singer	歌手 *複數：singers 歌手們
16	dancer	舞者 *複數：dancers 舞者們
17	like to	喜歡（後接原形動詞）
18	horse	馬
19	fish	魚

Unit 6

She Runs 她跑

| 1 | run | 跑 |

*runs: run 的第三人稱單數現在式動詞

| 2 | sing | 唱 |

*sings: sing 的第三人稱單數現在式動詞

| 3 | dance | 跳舞 |

*dances: dance 的第三人稱單數現在式動詞

| 4 | swim | 游泳 |

*swims: swim 的第三人稱單數現在式動詞

| 5 | like to | 喜歡 |

*likes to: like to 的第三人稱單數現在式動詞

6	meet	認識
7	my friend	我的朋友
8	name	名字
9	fun	有趣的；愉快的

Unit 7

Go, Went
去（go 的現在式），
去（go 的過去式）

1	school	學校
2	park	公園
3	movie	電影
4	party	派對
5	come home	回家
6	do homework	做功課
7	play baseball	打棒球

8	eat	吃
9	ate	吃 *eat 的過去式
10	apple	蘋果
11	banana	香蕉
12	sandwich	三明治
13	cookie	餅乾
14	today	今天
15	yesterday	昨天
16	too	也
17	go	去
18	went	去 *go 的過去式
19	go to school	上學
20	go to the park	去公園
21	go to a movie	去看電影
22	go to a party	去派對
23	do	做
24	did	做 *do 的過去式
25	come	來
26	came	來 *come 的過去式
27	see	看見
28	saw	看見 *see 的過去式
29	play	玩
30	played	玩 *play 的過去式
31	busy	忙碌的

Unit 8

Will, Be Going to
將要，即將要去

1	play soccer	踢足球
2	play baseball	打棒球
3	play a game	玩遊戲
4	play with friends	跟朋友一起玩
5	ride	騎
6	ride a bike	騎腳踏車
7	watch	觀看；注視
8	watch TV	看電視
9	have a party	舉辦派對
10	will	將要
11	tomorrow	明天
12	be going to	即將要去……
13	birthday	生日
14	birthday party	生日派對

國家圖書館出版品預行編目資料

FUN 學美國各學科 Preschool 閱讀課本 . 1, 動詞篇（寂天隨身聽 APP 版）/
Michael A. Putlack, e-Creative Contents 著 . -- 二版 . -- [臺北市]：寂天文化 , 2021.09
　面；　公分
ISBN 978-626-300-020-9(菊 8K 平裝)

1. 英語 2. 動詞

805.165　　　　　　　　　　　　　　　　　　　110008448

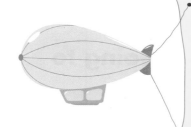

FUN學 美國各學科
Preschool 閱讀課本 1 二版

Preschool
動詞篇

作　　者	Michael A. Putlack & e-Creative Contents
譯　　者	歐寶妮
編　　輯	林晨禾／歐寶妮
主　　編	丁宥暄
內文排版	林書玉（課本）／謝青秀（練習本）
封面設計	林書玉
製程管理	洪巧玲
出 版 者	寂天文化事業股份有限公司
發 行 人	黃朝萍
電　　話	02-2365-9739
傳　　真	02-2365-9835
網　　址	www.icosmos.com.tw
讀者服務	onlineservice@icosmos.com.tw
出版日期	2023 年 9 月　二版再刷　（寂天雲隨身聽 APP 版）（0202）

郵撥帳號　1998620-0　寂天文化事業股份有限公司
訂書金額未滿 1000 元，請外加運費 100 元。
〔若有破損，請寄回更換，謝謝〕

FUN學美國各學科

Preschool 閱讀課本 二版

AMERiCAN SCHOOL TEXTBOOK

Reading Key

1

Preschool
動詞篇

WORKBOOK
練習本

Workbook

1 I Am, I Have

A Read and write.

1.  lion

lion

2.  elephant

elephant

3.  giraffe

giraffe

4.  hippo

hippo

B Match and write.

1. trunk   trunk

2. mane   mane

3. neck   neck

4. mouth   mouth

5. hands   hands

6. legs   legs

C Circle the correct word for each sentence.

1.

   I am a (**hippo**, **giraffe**).

2.

   I am an (**elephant, lion**).

3.

   I am a (**giraffe, lion**).

4.

   I am a (**lion, elephant**).

D Choose and write.

hands	neck	ears	mane	trunk	mouth

1.

   I have two ___**hands**___.

2.

   I have two _____.

3.

   I have a _____.

4.

   I have a long _____.

5.

   I have a big _____.

6.

   I have a _____.

2 He Is, He Has

A Read and write.

1.

boy   he

boy   he

2.

girl   she

girl   she

3.

cat   dog   rabbit   bird

cat   dog   rabbit   bird

B Match and write.

1. it   it

2. she   she

3. he   he

4. wings   wings

5. ears   ears

6. eyes   eyes

Circle the correct word for each sentence.

1.

The boy (**is**, **has**) Tom.

2.

He (**is**, **has**) John.

3.

The girl (**is**, **has**) Jane.

4.

She (**is**, **has**) Julie.

D **Choose and write.**

eyes	ears	mouth	wings

1.

It has big __eyes__ .

2.

It has a big _____ .

3.

It has two _____ .

4.

It has long _____ .

3 I Am Running

A Read and write.

1.

walk | run

walk   run

2.

fly | swim

fly   swim

3.

sing | dance

sing   dance

4.

cook | eat

cook   eat

B Match and write.

1. walking   walking

2. running   running

3. flying   flying

4. swimming   swimming

5. singing   singing

6. dancing   dancing

C Circle the correct word for each sentence.

1.

I am (**walking**, **running**).

2.

I am (**walking**, **running**).

3.

I am (**swimming**, **flying**).

4.

I am (**swimming**, **flying**).

D Choose and write.

| eating | dancing | cooking | singing |

1.

The girl is ___singing___.

2.

The boy is _____.

3.

Mom is _____.

4.

Tom is _____.

You Are Sleeping

A Read and write.

1.

I
I

you
you

we
we

2.

he
he

she
she

they
they

B Match and write.

1. friends   friends

2. children   children

3. eat   eat

4. drink   drink

5. sleep   sleep

6. jump   jump

Circle the correct word for each sentence.

1.

I (**am**, **are**) Ann.

2.

You (**am**, **are**) Tom.

3.

We (**is**, **are**) friends.

4.

They (**is**, **are**) children.

5.

He (**is**, **are**) a boy.

6.

She (**is**, **are**) a girl.

D **Choose and write.**

jumping   eating   drinking   sleeping

1.

I am ___eating___ pizza.

2.

You are _____ milk.

3.

We are _____ together.

4.

They are _____.

5 I Run

A Read and write.

1.  rabbit
rabbit

2.  turtle
turtle

3.  frog
frog

4.  dolphin
dolphin

B Match and write.

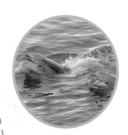

1. I run.
I run.

2. You walk.
You walk.

3. We jump.
We jump.

4. They swim.
They swim.

12

C Circle the correct word for each sentence.

1.

   I am a rabbit.
   I (**run**, **swim**) fast.

2.

   You are a turtle.
   You (**walk**, **sing**) slowly.

3.

   We are frogs.
   We (**jump**, **sing**) well.

4.

   They are dolphins.
   They (**swim**, **run**) well.

D Choose and write.

sing	run	like	swim

1.

   I __like__ to dance.
   I dance well.

2.

   I like to sing.
   I _____ well.

3.

   I like to run.
   I _____ fast.

4.

   I like to swim.
   I _____ well.

6 She Runs

A Read and write.

1.

she	he	it
she	he	it

2.

She runs.   It sings.

She runs.   It sings.

B Match and write.

1. She sings well.

She sings well.

2. He dances well.

He dances well.

3. It swims fast.

It swims fast.

4. It runs fast.

It runs fast.

C Circle the correct word for each sentence.

1.

I see a girl.
She (**sing**, **sings**) well.

2.

I see a boy.
He (**dance**, **dances**) well.

3.

I see a fish.
It (**swim**, **swims**) fast.

4.

I see a horse.
It (**run**, **runs**) fast.

D Choose and write.

likes	eats	jumps	dances

1. He __**likes**__ to run.
   He runs fast.

2. He likes to jump.
   He _____ well.

3. He likes to dance.
   He _____ well.

4. He likes to eat.
   He _____ well.

7 Go, Went

A Read and write.

1.  school

   school

2.  park

   park

3.  movie

   movie

4.  party

   party

B Match and write.

1. come home   come home 

2. go to school   go to school 

3. do homework   do homework

4. play baseball   play baseball

5. see a bird   see a bird

6. eat an apple   eat an apple

C Circle the correct word for each sentence.

1.

Yesterday, I (**go, went**) to school.

2.

Yesterday, I (**come, came**) home early.

3.

Yesterday, I (**eat, ate**) an apple.

4.

Yesterday, I (**do, did**) my homework.

5.

Yesterday, I (**see, saw**) a bird.

6.

Yesterday, I (**play, played**) baseball.

D Choose and write.

went to	saw	played	ate

1.

Yesterday, I ___saw___ a bird.
I _____ baseball.

2.

Yesterday, I _____ a party.
I _____ cake.

8 Will, Be Going to

A Read and write.

1.  soccer

   soccer

2.  baseball

   baseball

3.  bike

   bike

4.  birthday

   birthday

B Match and write.

1. play soccer

   play soccer

2. play a game

   play a game

3. play with friends

   play with friends

4. ride a bike

   ride a bike

5. watch TV

   watch TV

6. have a party

   have a party

C Circle the correct word for each sentence.

1.  Tomorrow, I will (**play**, **played**) soccer.

2.  Tomorrow, you will (**go**, **went**) to school.

3.  Tomorrow, I am (**go**, **going**) to go to the park.

4.  Tomorrow, you are going to (**play**, **played**) a game.

D Choose and write.

| eat | have | come | going to | play |

1. Tomorrow, I will ___have___ a party.

2. My friends will _____ to my party.

3. We are _____ eat cake.

4. We are going to _____ pizza.

5. We are going to _____ a game.

Textbook Answers and Translations

課本解答與翻譯

22 Textbook Answers and Translations

Am or Have? 「是」或「有」？
圈出每個句子中正確的單字。

 Who Am I? 我是誰？
將每組句子連接到正確的動物。

I am a lion.
I (am, **have**) a mane.
我是一隻獅子。
我（是；有）鬃毛。

I am a giraffe.
I (am, **have**) a long neck.
我是一隻長頸鹿。
我（是；有）長脖子。

I am an elephant.
I (am, **have**) a trunk.
我是一隻大象。
我（是；有）象鼻。

I am a hippo.
I (**am**, have) a big mouth.
我是一頭河馬。
我（是；有）大嘴巴。

I have four legs.
I have a long neck.
我有四隻腳。
我有長脖子。

I have four legs.
I have a trunk.
我有四隻腳。
我有象鼻。

I have four legs.
I have a mane.
我有四隻腳。
我有鬃毛。

I have four legs.
I have a big mouth.
我有四隻腳。
我有大嘴巴。

elephant 大象

lion 獅子

giraffe 長頸鹿

hippo 河馬

10

I Can Read 我會閱讀
閱讀故事，並圈出每個句子中正確的單字。

Animals in Africa
在非洲的動物

I am an elephant.
I have a (**trunk**, mane).
我是一隻大象。
我有（象鼻；鬃毛）。

I am a lion.
I have a (**mane**, trunk).
我是一隻獅子。
我有（鬃毛；象鼻）。

I am a hippo.
I have a big (**mouth**, mane).
我是一隻河馬。
我有大（嘴巴；鬃毛）。

I am a giraffe.
I have a long (**neck**, trunk).
我是一隻長頸鹿。
我有長（脖子；象鼻）。

12

13

UNIT 2 He Is, He Has
他是；他有

Key Words 關鍵字彙
閱讀以下單字。

boy = he
男孩＝他

girl = she
女孩＝她

bird 鳥

rabbit 兔子

it 牠

dog 狗

cat 貓

14
15

他是；她是；牠是
He Is, She Is, It Is
圈出單字「is」。

The boy is Tom.
這個男孩是湯姆。

He is John.
他是約翰。

The girl is Jane.
這個女孩是珍。

She is Julie.
她是茱莉。

It is a bird.
牠是一隻鳥。

他有；她有；牠有
He Has, She Has, It Has
圈出單字「has」。

- The girl has a cat.
- She has a cat.
- 女孩有一隻貓。
- 她有一隻貓。

- The boy has a dog.
- He has a dog.
- 男孩有一隻狗。
- 他有一隻狗。

- The girl has a rabbit.
- She has a rabbit.
- 女孩有一隻兔子。
- 她有一隻兔子。

- The boy has a bird.
- He has a bird.
- 男孩有一隻鳥。
- 他有一隻鳥。

- The bird has two wings.
- It has two wings.
- 小鳥有一對翅膀。
- 牠有一對翅膀。

16
17

Have or Has?
有（第一、二人稱）；有（第三人稱）
圈出每個句子中正確的字詞。

Who has the cat? 貓是誰的？
Jane (**have**, **has**) the cat. 貓是珍的。

Who has the dog? 狗是誰的？
Tom (**have**, **has**) the dog. 狗是湯姆的。

Who has the rabbit? 兔子是誰的？
Julie (**have**, **has**) the rabbit. 兔子是茱莉的。

Who has the bird? 鳥是誰的？
John (**have**, **has**) the bird. 鳥是約翰的。

Jane 珍
Tom 湯姆
Julie 茱莉
John 約翰

18

What Is It? 牠是什麼？
將每個句子連接到正確的動物。

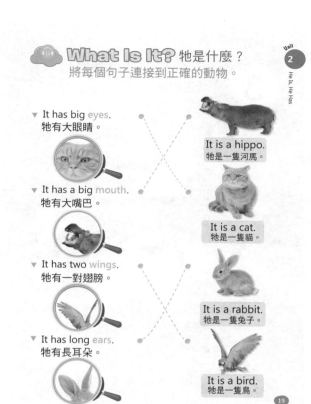

▼ It has big eyes.
牠有大眼睛。

▼ It has a big mouth.
牠有大嘴巴。

▼ It has two wings.
牠有一對翅膀。

▼ It has long ears.
牠有長耳朵。

It is a hippo.
牠是一隻河馬。

It is a cat.
牠是一隻貓。

It is a rabbit.
牠是一隻兔子。

It is a bird.
牠是一隻鳥。

19

I Can Read 我會閱讀
閱讀故事，並圈出句子中正確的字詞。

Animal Friends 動物朋友

(**She**, **He**) is Jane.
She has a cat.
It has big eyes.
（她；他）是珍。
她有一隻貓。
牠有大眼睛。

(**She**, **He**) is Jake.
He has a dog.
It has big ears.
（她；他）是傑克。
他有一隻狗。
牠有大耳朵。

She is Anna.
She (**has**, **have**) a bird.
It has two wings.
她是安娜。
她（有；有）一隻鳥。
牠有一對翅膀。

He is Tom.
He has a rabbit.
It (**has**, **have**) long ears.
他是湯姆。
他有一隻兔子。
牠（有；有）長耳朵。

20
21

I See 我看見……
在空格中填入正確的字詞。

| walking | running | swimming | flying |

I see a lion.
The lion is **walking**.

我看到一隻獅子。
那隻獅子正在走路。

I see a zebra.
The zebra is **running**.

我看到一隻斑馬。
那隻斑馬正在跑步。

I see a hippo.
The hippo is **swimming**.

我看到一隻河馬。
那隻河馬正在游泳。

I see a bird.
The bird is **flying**.

我看到一隻鳥。
那隻鳥正在飛。

26

正在唱歌；唱歌
Singing or Sing?
圈出句子中正確的字詞。

I see a girl.
The girl is (**singing**, sing).

我看到一個女孩。
女孩（正在唱歌；唱歌）。

I see a boy.
The boy is (**dancing**, dance).

我看到一個男孩。
男孩（正在跳舞；跳舞）。

I see Mom.
Mom is (cook, **cooking**).

我看到媽媽。
媽媽（煮飯；正在煮飯）。

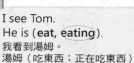

I see Tom.
He is (eat, **eating**).

我看到湯姆。
湯姆（吃東西；正在吃東西）。

27

I Can Read 我會閱讀
閱讀故事，並圈出每個句子中正確的字詞。

What is Ann **doing**?
She is (singing, **swimming**).

安正在做什麼？
她（正在唱歌；正在游泳）。

What is Tom **doing**?
He is (dancing, **running**).

湯姆正在做什麼？
他（正在跳舞；正在跑步）。

28

What is Mom **doing**?
She is (flying, **cooking**).

媽媽正在做什麼？
她（正在飛；正在煮飯）。

What is Ben **doing**?
He is (eating, **walking**).

班正在做什麼？
他（正在吃東西；正在走路）。

29

You Are Sleeping
你正在睡覺。

Key Words 關鍵字彙
閱讀以下單字。

I 我　you 你　we 我們

he 他　she 她　they 他們

eat 吃

drink 喝

sleep 睡覺　jump 跳

30 / 31

你是；他們是……

You Are, They Are
圈出字詞中的藍色部分。

I am Ann. 我是安。
You are Tom. 你是湯姆。
We are friends. 我們是朋友。

He is a boy. 他是男孩。
They are children. 他們是小孩。
She is a girl. 她是女孩。

You Are Doing 你正在……
圈出字詞中有「ing」的部分。

I am eating. 我正在吃。
You are drinking. 你正在喝。

We are jumping. 我們正在跳。
They are sleeping. 他們正在睡覺。

32 / 33

What Are You Doing?
你們正在做什麼？
圈出句子中正確的字詞。

 **What Are They Doing?**
牠們正在做什麼？
圈出句子中正確的字詞。

I am Ann.
I am (**eating**, drinking) pizza.
我是安。
我（正在吃；正在喝）披薩。

You are Tom.
You are (eating, **drinking**) milk.
你是湯姆。
你（正在吃；正在喝）牛奶。

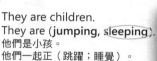
We are good friends.
We are (**jumping**, sleeping) together.
我們是好朋友。
我們正一起（跳躍；睡覺）。

They are children.
They are (jumping, **sleeping**).
他們是小孩。
他們一起正（跳躍；睡覺）。

I see lions.
They are (**sleeping**, jumping).
我看見獅子。
牠們（正在睡覺；正在跳）。

I see kangaroos.
They are (sleeping, **jumping**).
我看見袋鼠。
牠們（正在睡覺；正在跳）。

I see giraffes.
They are (**eating**, drinking) grass.
我看見長頸鹿。
牠們（正在吃；正在喝）草。

I see elephants.
They are (eating, **drinking**) water.
我看見大象。
牠們（正在吃；正在喝）水。

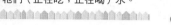

34 35

 I Can Read 我會閱讀
閱讀故事，並圈出每個句子中正確的單字。

What are you **doing**?
I am (eat, **eating**) ice cream.
你正在做什麼？
我（吃；正在吃）
冰淇淋。

What are you **doing**?
I am (drink, **drinking**) milk.
你正在做什麼？
我（喝；正在喝）牛奶。

What are they **doing**?
They are (sleep, **sleeping**).
他們正在做什麼？
他們（睡覺；正在睡覺）。

What are they **doing**?
They are (jump, **jumping**) rope.
他們正在做什麼？
他們（跳；正在跳）繩。

36 37

29

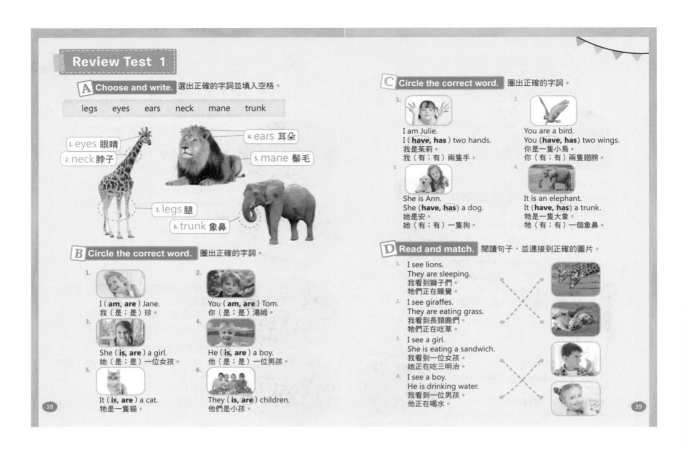

Review Test 1

A **Choose and write.** 選出正確的字詞並填入空格。

legs eyes ears neck mane trunk

1. eyes 眼睛
2. neck 脖子
3. legs 腿
4. ears 耳朵
5. mane 鬃毛
6. trunk 象鼻

B **Circle the correct word.** 圈出正確的字詞。

1. I (**am**, are) Jane.
   我（是；是）珍。
2. You (**am**, **are**) Tom.
   你（是；是）湯姆。
3. She (**is**, are) a girl.
   她（是；是）一位女孩。
4. He (**is**, are) a boy.
   他（是；是）一位男孩。
5. It (**is**, are) a cat.
   牠是一隻貓。
6. They (is, **are**) children.
   他們是小孩。

C **Circle the correct word.** 圈出正確的字詞。

1. I am Julie.
   I (**have**, has) two hands.
   我是茱莉。
   我（有；有）兩隻手。
2. You are a bird.
   You (**have**, has) two wings.
   你是一隻小鳥。
   你（有；有）兩隻翅膀。
3. She is Ann.
   She (have, **has**) a dog.
   她是安。
   她（有；有）一隻狗。
4. It is an elephant.
   It (have, **has**) a trunk.
   牠是一隻大象。
   牠（有；有）一個象鼻。

D **Read and match.** 閱讀句子，並連接到正確的圖片。

1. I see lions.
   They are sleeping.
   我看到獅子們。
   牠們正在睡覺。
2. I see giraffes.
   They are eating grass.
   我看到長頸鹿們。
   牠們正在吃草。
3. I see a girl.
   She is eating a sandwich.
   我看到一位女孩。
   她正在吃三明治。
4. I see a boy.
   He is drinking water.
   我看到一位男孩。
   他正在喝水。

UNIT 5

I Run 我跑

Key Words 關鍵單字
閱讀以下單字與句子。

rabbit 兔子

turtle 烏龜

frog 菁蛙

dolphin 海豚

I run. 我跑。

You walk. 你走。

We jump. 我們跳。

They swim. 牠們游泳。

Unit 5 I Run

Who Are You? 你是誰？
圈出字詞中的藍色部分。

I am a rabbit.
我是一隻兔子。

You are a turtle.
你是一隻烏龜。

We are frogs.
我們是青蛙。

They are dolphins.
牠們是海豚。

跑步；跳躍；游泳
Run, Jump, Swim
圈出字詞中的藍色部分。

I am a rabbit. 我是一隻兔子。
I run fast. 我跑得很快。

You are a turtle. 你是一隻烏龜。
You walk slowly. 你走得很慢。

We are frogs. 我們是青蛙。
We jump well. 我們很會跳。

They are dolphins. 牠們是海豚。
They swim well. 牠們很會游泳。

42

43

Sing, Dance 唱歌；跳舞
圈出句子中正確的字詞。

I am a singer.
I (sing, dance) well.
我是一位歌手。
我（唱得；跳得）很好。

You are a dancer.
You (sing, dance) well.
你是一名舞者。
你（唱得；跳得）很好。

We are singers.
We (sing, dance) well.
我們是歌手。
我們（唱得；跳得）很好。

They are dancers.
They (sing, dance) well.
他們是舞者。
他們（唱得；跳得）很好。

44

I Like to 我喜歡……
將圖片連接到敘述正確的句子。

I like to sing.
我喜歡唱歌。

I am a singer.
我是一位歌手。

I like to dance.
我喜歡跳舞。

I am a dancer.
我是一位舞者。

I like to swim.
我喜歡游泳。

I am a frog.
我是一隻青蛙。

I like to jump.
我喜歡跳。

I am a dolphin.
我是一隻海豚。

45

閱讀故事，並圈出句子中正確的字詞。

I Can Read 我會閱讀

Who Am I?
我是誰？

I like to dance.
I dance well.
I am a (dancer, singer).

我喜歡跳舞。
我跳得很好。
我是一位（舞者；歌手）。

I like to sing.
I sing well.
I am a (singer, dancer).

我喜歡唱歌。
我唱得很好。
我是一位（歌手；舞者）

I like to run.
I (run, swim) fast.
I am a horse.

我喜歡跑步。
我（跑得；游得）很快。
我是一隻馬。

I like to swim.
I (swim, run) well.
I am a fish.

我喜歡游泳。
我很會（游泳；跑）。
我是一隻魚。

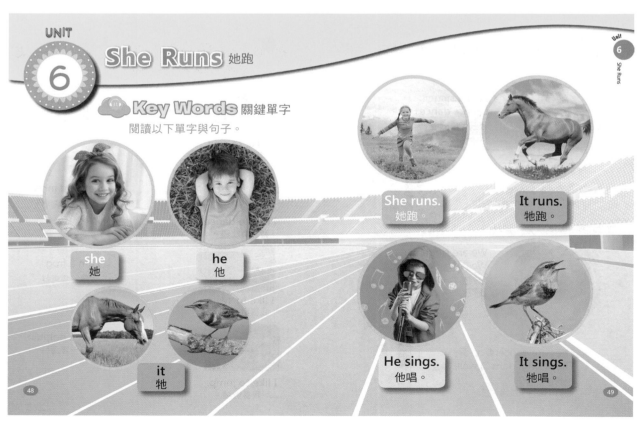

UNIT 6 She Runs 她跑

Key Words 關鍵單字
閱讀以下單字與句子。

she
她

he
他

it
牠

She runs.
她跑。

It runs.
牠跑。

He sings.
他唱。

It sings.
牠唱。

I See 我看到……

圈出字詞中的藍色部分。

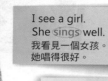

I see a girl.
She sings well.
我看見一個女孩。
她唱得很好。

I see a boy.
He dances well.
我看見一個男孩。
他舞跳得很好。

I see a dolphin.
It swims fast.
我看見一隻海豚。
牠游得很快。

I see a horse.
It runs fast.
我看見一隻馬。
牠跑得很快。

50

Sings, Dances 唱歌；跳舞

圈出句子中正確的字詞。

Unit 6 She Runs

The girl sings.
She (sing, **sings**) well.
女孩在唱歌。
她（唱得；唱得）很好。

The boy dances.
He (dance, **dances**) well.
男孩在跳舞。
他（跳得；跳得）很好。

The horse runs.
It (run, **runs**) fast.
馬在奔馳。
牠（跑得；跑得）很快。

The dolphin swims.
It (swim, **swims**) fast.
海豚在游泳。
牠（游得；游得）很快。

51

She Likes to 她喜歡……

將句子連接到敘述正確的圖片。

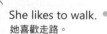

She likes to walk.
她喜歡走路。

He likes to run.
他喜歡跑步。

She likes to swim.
她喜歡游泳。

He likes to sleep.
他喜歡睡覺。

It likes to jump.
牠喜歡跳。

52

Who Are They? 他們是誰？

圈出句子中正確的字詞。

Unit 6 She Runs

She is Jane.
She (like, **likes**) to walk.
她是珍。
她喜歡走路。

He is Tom.
He (like, **likes**) to run.
他是湯姆。
他喜歡跑步。

The girl is Ann.
She (like, **likes**) to swim.
這個女孩是安。
她喜歡游泳。

It is a cat.
It (like, **likes**) to sleep.
牠是一隻貓。
牠喜歡睡覺。

It is a frog.
It (like, **likes**) to jump.
牠是一隻青蛙。
牠喜歡跳。

53

33

I Can Read 我會閱讀

閱讀故事，並圈出句子中正確的字詞。

Meet My Friend
認識我的朋友

I have a dog.
His name is Sam.
我有一隻狗。
他的名字叫山姆。

He likes to run.
He (**run**, **runs**) fast.
他喜歡跑步。
他（跑得；跑得）很快。

He likes to jump.
He (**jump**, **jumps**) well.
他喜歡跳。
他很會（跳；跳）。

He likes to dance.
He (**dance**, **dances**) well.
他喜歡跳舞。
他舞（跳得；跳得）很好。

He likes to eat.
He (**eat**, **eats**) well.
He is fun.
他喜歡吃。
他很會（吃；吃）。
他很有趣。

54

55

UNIT 7

go（去）的現在式；go（去）的過去式

Go, Went

Key Words 關鍵單字

閱讀以下字詞。

come home
回家

do homework
做作業

play baseball
打棒球

school 學校

park 公園

movie 電影

party 派對

56

57

eat（吃）的現在式；eat（吃）的過去式

Eat, Ate
圈出單字「eat」，在單字「ate」底下劃線。

Today 今天	Yesterday 昨天
I eat an apple. 我吃一顆蘋果。	I ate an apple. 我吃了一顆蘋果。
I eat a banana. 我吃一根香蕉。	I ate a banana. 我吃了一根香蕉。
I eat a sandwich. 我吃一個三明治。	I ate a sandwich. 我吃了一個三明治。
I eat a cookie. 我吃一片餅乾。	I ate a cookie. 我吃了一片餅乾。

58

eat 的現在式或過去式？

Eat or Ate?
圈出句子中正確的字詞。

Today, I eat an apple.
Yesterday, I (**eat**, **ate**) an apple, too.
今天，我吃一顆蘋果。
昨天，我也（吃；吃了）一顆蘋果。

Today, I eat a banana.
Yesterday, I (**eat**, **ate**) a banana, too.
今天，我吃一根香蕉。
昨天，我也（吃；吃了）一根香蕉。

Today, I eat a sandwich.
Yesterday, I (**eat**, **ate**) a sandwich, too.
今天，我吃一個三明治。
昨天，我也（吃；吃了）一個三明治。

Today, I eat a cookie.
Yesterday, I (**eat**, **ate**) a cookie, too.
今天，我吃一片餅乾。
昨天，我也（吃；吃了）一片餅乾。

59

---

go（去）的現在式；go（去）的過去式

Go, Went
圈出單字「go」，在單字「went」底下劃線

Today 今天		Yesterday 昨天
I go to school. 我去上學。		I went to school. 我去上了學。
I go to the park. 我去公園。		I went to the park. 我去了公園。
I go to a movie. 我去看電影。		I went to a movie. 我去看了電影。
I go to a party. 我去派對。		I went to a party. 我去了派對。

60

go 的現在式或過去式？

Go or Went?
圈出句子中正確的字詞。

Today, I go to school.
Yesterday, I (**go**, **went**) to school, too.
今天，我去上學。
昨天，我也（去；去了）學校。

Today, I go to the park.
Yesterday, I (**go**, **went**) to the park, too.
今天，我去公園。
昨天，我也（去；去了）公園。

Today, I go to a movie.
Yesterday, I (**go**, **went**) to a movie, too.
今天，我去看電影。
昨天，我也去（看；看了）電影。

Today, I go to a party.
Yesterday, I (**go**, **went**) to a party, too.
今天，我去派對。
昨天，我也（去；去了）派對。

61

do（做）的現在式；do（做）的過去式

Do, Did
圈出字詞中藍色的部分，在紅色部分底下劃線

do 的現在式或過去式？

Do or Did?
圈出句子中正確的字詞。

Today 今天	Yesterday 昨天
I do my homework. 我寫我的功課。	I did my homework. 我寫了我的功課。
I come home early. 我很早回家。	I came home early. 我很早回家。
I see a bird. 我看到一隻鳥。	I saw a bird. 我看到了一隻鳥。
I play baseball. 我打棒球。	I played baseball. 我打了棒球。

Today, I do my homework.
Yesterday, I (do, **did**) my homework, too.
今天，我寫我的功課。
昨天，我也（寫；寫了）我的功課。

Today, I come home early.
Yesterday, I (come, **came**) home early, too.
今天，我很早回家。
昨天，我也很早（回；回了）家。

Today, I see a bird.
Yesterday, I (see, **saw**) a bird, too.
今天，我看到一隻鳥。
昨天，我也（看到；看到了）一隻鳥。

Today, I play baseball.
Yesterday, I (play, **played**) baseball, too.
今天，我打棒球。
昨天，我也（打；打了）棒球。

62

63

I Can Read 我會閱讀
閱讀故事，並圈出字詞中的藍色部分。

Yesterday, I was busy.
昨天，我很忙。

I went to school.
我去了學校。

I went to the park.
我去了公園。

I played baseball.
我打了棒球。

I went to a party.
我去了派對。

I ate cake.
I ate pizza.
I ate ice cream.
I ate a cookie, too.

我吃了蛋糕。
我吃了披薩。
我吃了冰淇淋。
我也吃了餅乾。

64

65

UNIT 8

Will, Be Going to
將；即將要

Key Words 關鍵單字
閱讀以下字詞。

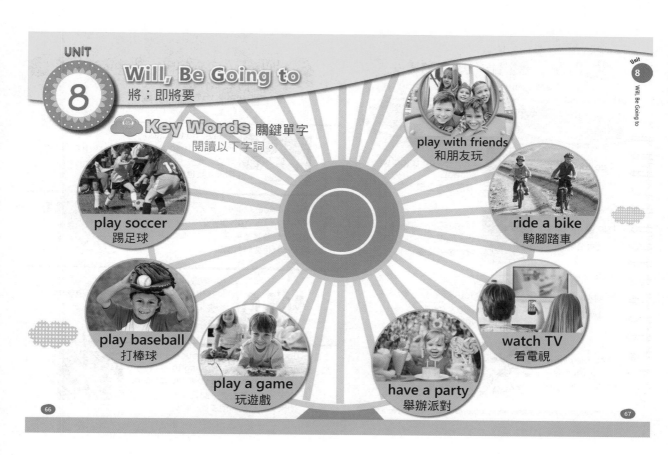

play with friends
和朋友玩

ride a bike
騎腳踏車

play soccer
踢足球

play baseball
打棒球

play a game
玩遊戲

have a party
舉辦派對

watch TV
看電視

66 67

I Will 我將會……
圈出單字「will」。

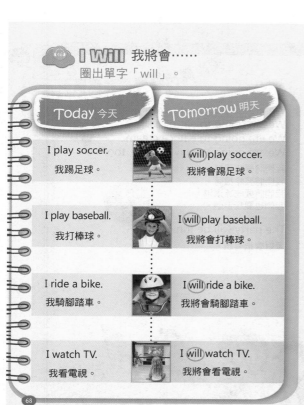

Today 今天	Tomorrow 明天
I play soccer. 我踢足球。	I will play soccer. 我將會踢足球。
I play baseball. 我打棒球。	I will play baseball. 我將會打棒球。
I ride a bike. 我騎腳踏車。	I will ride a bike. 我將會騎腳踏車。
I watch TV. 我看電視。	I will watch TV. 我將會看電視。

68

你將做什麼？
What Will You Do?
圈出單字「will」。

Today, I play soccer.
Tomorrow, I will play soccer, too.
今天，我踢足球。
明天，我也會踢足球。

Today, you play baseball.
Tomorrow, you will play baseball, too.
今天，你打棒球。
明天，你也會打棒球。

Today, we ride a bike.
Tomorrow, we will ride a bike, too.
今天，我們騎腳踏車。
明天，我們也會騎腳踏車。

Today, they watch TV.
Tomorrow, they will watch TV, too.
今天，他們看電視。
明天，他們也會看電視。

69

I Am Going to 我將要……
圈出「am going to」和「are going to」。

Today 今天		Tomorrow 明天
I go to school. 我去上學。		I am going to go to school. 我將要去上學。
I go to the park. 我去公園。		I am going to go to the park. 我將要去公園。
You play a game. 你玩遊戲。		You are going to play a game. 你將要玩遊戲。
You play with your friends. 你和朋友們一起玩。		You are going to play with your friends. 你將要和朋友們一起玩。

70

What Are You Going to Do?
你將要做什麼？
圈出句子中正確的字詞。

Today, I go to school.
Tomorrow, I (am, are) going to go to school, too.
今天，我去上學。
明天，我也要去上學。

Today, I ride a bike.
Tomorrow, I am (go, going) to ride a bike, too.
今天，我騎腳踏車。
明天，我也要騎腳踏車。

Today, you play a game.
Tomorrow, you are (go, going) to play a game, too.
今天，你玩遊戲。
明天，你也要玩遊戲。

Today, you play with your friends.
Tomorrow, you are going to
(play, played) with your friends, too.
今天，你和朋友們一起玩。
明天，你也要和朋友們一起玩。

71

I Can Read 我會閱讀
圈出「will」和「are going to」。

My Birthday Party
我的生日派對

Tomorrow is my birthday.
I will have a party.
明天是我的生日。
我將舉辦一個派對。

My friends will come to my party.
Jane will come to my party.
Tina will come to my party.
Ben will come to my party, too.
我的朋友們會參加我的派對。
珍會參加我的派對。
蒂娜會參加我的派對。
班也會參加我的派對。

72

We are going to eat cake.
We are going to eat pizza.
We are going to eat ice cream.
We are going to play a game, too.
我們將要吃蛋糕。
我們將要吃披薩。
我們將要吃冰淇淋。
我們也要玩遊戲。

The party will be fun.
派對會很有趣。

73

Review Test 2

A Choose and write. 選出正確的字詞並填入空格。

jump   run   swim   walk   dance   sing

1. run 跑

 2. walk 走路

3. jump 跳

 4. swim 游泳

5. sing 唱歌

 6. dance 跳舞

B Circle the correct word. 圈出正確的字詞。

1.
I (**run, runs**) fast.
我（跑得；跑得）很快。

2.
You (**walk, walks**) slowly.
你（走得；走得）很慢。

3.
We (**sing, sings**) well.
我們（唱得；唱得）不錯。

4.
They (**dance, dances**) well.
他們舞（跳得；跳得）不錯。

5.
He (**jump, jumps**) well.
他（跳得；跳得）很好。

6.
It (**swim, swims**) fast.
牠（游得；游得）很快。

C Circle the correct word. 圈出正確的字詞。

1.
I (**like, likes**) to dance.
I am a dancer.
我（喜歡；喜歡）跳舞。
我是一名舞者。

2.
You (**like, likes**) to sing.
You are a singer.
你（喜歡；喜歡）唱歌。
你是一位歌手。

3.
He (**like, likes**) to run.
He runs fast.
他（喜歡；喜歡）跑步。
他跑得很快。

4.
It (**like, likes**) to swim.
It swims well.
牠（喜歡；喜歡）游泳。
牠游得很好。

D Choose and match. 圈出正確的字詞，並連接到正確的圖片。

1. Today, I come home early.
Yesterday, I (**come, came**) home early, too.
今天，我很早回家。
昨天，我也很早（回；回了）家。

2. Today, I see a bird.
Yesterday, I (**see, saw**) a bird, too.
今天，我看見一隻小鳥。
昨天，我也（看見；看見了）一隻小鳥。

3. Today, I play soccer.
Tomorrow, I will (**play, played**) soccer, too.
今天，我玩足球。
明天，我也會（玩；玩了）足球。

4. Today, I eat cake.
Tomorrow, I am going to (**eat, ate**) cake, too.
今天，我吃蛋糕。
明天，我也會（吃；吃了）蛋糕。

Daily Test Answers

課堂練習解答

1 I Am, I Have

A Read and write.

1. lion

   lion

2. elephant

   elephant

3. giraffe

   giraffe

4. hippo

   hippo

B Match and write.

1. trunk — trunk
2. mane — mane
3. neck — neck
4. mouth — mouth
5. hands — hands
6. legs — legs

C Circle the correct word for each sentence.

1. I am a (**hippo**, giraffe).
2. I am an (**elephant**, lion).
3. I am a (**giraffe**, lion).
4. I am a (**lion**, elephant).

D Choose and write.

hands   neck   ears   mane   trunk   mouth

1. I have two __hands__.
2. I have two __ears__.
3. I have a __mane__.
4. I have a long __neck__.
5. I have a big __mouth__.
6. I have a __trunk__.

2 He Is, He Has

A Read and write.

1.

   boy   he

   boy   he

2. girl   she

   girl   she

3.

   cat   dog   rabbit   bird

   cat   dog   rabbit   bird

B Match and write.

1. it — it
2. she — she
3. he — he
4. wings — wings
5. ears — ears
6. eyes — eyes

C Circle the correct word for each sentence.

1. The boy (**is**, has) Tom.
2. He (**is**, has) John.
3. The girl (**is**, has) Jane.
4. She (**is**, has) Julie.

D Choose and write.

eyes   ears   mouth   wings

1. It has big __eyes__.
2. It has a big __mouth__.
3. It has two __wings__.
4. It has long __ears__.

3 I Am Running

A Read and write.

1.
walk   run

walk   run

2.
fly   swim

fly   swim

3.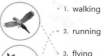
sing   dance

sing   dance

4.
cook   eat

cook   eat

B Match and write.

1. walking   walking
2. running   running
3. flying   flying
4. swimming   swimming
5. singing   singing
6. dancing   dancing

C Circle the correct word for each sentence.

1.
I am (**walking**, running).

2.
I am (walking, **running**).

3.
I am (**swimming**, flying).

4.
I am (**swimming**, flying).

D Choose and write.

eating   dancing   cooking   singing

1.
The girl is __singing__.

2.
The boy is __dancing__.

3.
Mom is __cooking__.

4.
Tom is __eating__.

---

4 You Are Sleeping

A Read and write.

1.
I   you   we

I   you   we

2.
he   she   they

he   she   they

B Match and write.

1. friends   friends
2. children   children
3. eat   eat
4. drink   drink
5. sleep   sleep
6. jump   jump

C Circle the correct word for each sentence.

1.
I (**am**, are) Ann.

2.
You (am, **are**) Tom.

3.
We (is, **are**) friends.

4.
They (is, **are**) children.

5.
He (**is**, are) a boy.

6.
She (**is**, are) a girl.

D Choose and write.

jumping   eating   drinking   sleeping

1.
I am __eating__ pizza.

2.
You are __drinking__ milk.

3.
We are __jumping__ together.

4.
They are __sleeping__.

5 I Run

A Read and write.

1. rabbit

rabbit

2. turtle

turtle

3. frog

frog

4. dolphin

dolphin

B Match and write.

1. I run.

I run.

2. You walk.

You walk.

3. We jump.

We jump.

4. They swim.

They swim.

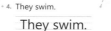

C Circle the correct word for each sentence.

1.

I am a rabbit.
I (**run**, swim) fast.

2.

You are a turtle.
You (**walk**, sing) slowly.

3.

We are frogs.
We (**jump**, sing) well.

4.

They are dolphins.
They (**swim**, run) well.

D Choose and write.

sing	run	like	swim

1.

I __like__ to dance.
I dance well.

2.

I like to sing.
I __sing__ well.

3.

I like to run.
I __run__ fast.

4.

I like to swim.
I __swim__ well.

---

6 She Runs

A Read and write.

1. she   he   it

she   he   it

2. She runs.   It sings.

She runs.   It sings.

B Match and write.

1. She sings well.

She sings well.

2. He dances well.

He dances well.

3. It swims fast.

It swims fast.

4. It runs fast.

It runs fast.

C Circle the correct word for each sentence.

1.

I see a girl.
She (sing, **sings**) well.

2.

I see a boy.
He (dance, **dances**) well.

3.

I see a fish.
It (swim, **swims**) fast.

4.

I see a horse.
It (run, **runs**) fast.

D Choose and write.

likes	eats	jumps	dances

1. He __likes__ to run.
He runs fast.

2. He likes to jump.
He __jumps__ well.

3. He likes to dance.
He __dances__ well.

4. He likes to eat.
He __eats__ well.

7 Go, Went

A Read and write.

1. school
school

2. park
park

3. movie
movie

4. party
party

B Match and write.

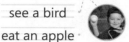

1. come home   come home
2. go to school   go to school
3. do homework   do homework
4. play baseball   play baseball
5. see a bird   see a bird
6. eat an apple   eat an apple

C Circle the correct word for each sentence.

1. Yesterday, I (**go**, **went**) to school.

2. Yesterday, I (**come**, **came**) home early.

3. Yesterday, I (**eat**, **ate**) an apple.

4. Yesterday, I (**do**, **did**) my homework.

5. Yesterday, I (**see**, **saw**) a bird.

6. Yesterday, I (**play**, **played**) baseball.

D Choose and write.

| went to | saw | played | ate |

1.   Yesterday, I __saw__ a bird. I __played__ baseball.

2.   Yesterday, I __went to__ a party. I __ate__ cake.

16   17

---

8 Will, Be Going to

A Read and write.

1. soccer
soccer

2. baseball
baseball

3. bike
bike

4. birthday
birthday

B Match and write.

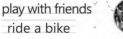

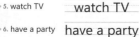

1. play soccer   play soccer
2. play a game   play a game
3. play with friends   play with friends
4. ride a bike   ride a bike
5. watch TV   watch TV
6. have a party   have a party

C Circle the correct word for each sentence.

1. Tomorrow, I will (**play**, **played**) soccer.

2. Tomorrow, you will (**go**, **went**) to school.

3. Tomorrow, I am (**go**, **going**) to go to the park.

4. Tomorrow, you are going to (**play**, **played**) a game.

D Choose and write.

| eat | have | come | going to | play |

1. Tomorrow, I will __have__ a party.

2. My friends will __come__ to my party.

3. We are __going to__ eat cake.

4. We are going to __eat__ pizza.

5. We are going to __play__ a game.

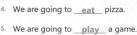

18   19